Little Billy

and

Baseball Bob

Written by Mitchell Axelrod
Illustrated by Ron Campbell

Wynn Publishing

www.littlebillyandbaseballbob.com

ISBN 0-9710591-2-8

Library of Congress Control Number: 2002110241

Published by Wynn Publishing
P.O. Box 1491
Pickens, SC 29671
(864) 878-6469

Printed in the United States of America

First Printing: January 2003

Book Design and Layout by Mitchell Axelrod and Diana Thornton

Little Billy loved baseball.

Little Billy loved baseball so much that he collected baseball cards and banners of all of the teams. He loved to play catch with his Dad whenever possible.

Every night Little Billy put on his
baseball pajamas and went to sleep in
his bed, which was shaped liked a big
baseball glove.

Above Little Billy's bed was what he called his "Wall of Favorite Pictures." On this wall were pictures of his Mom and Dad, Grandma and Grandpa, and even his dog Spot.

There was one empty spot on Billy's wall.

"I'm saving that spot for a picture of Baseball Bob, my favorite baseball player," Little Billy always told everyone.

Nice G

Baseball Bob played
for the Niceguys
and was a very
popular player.

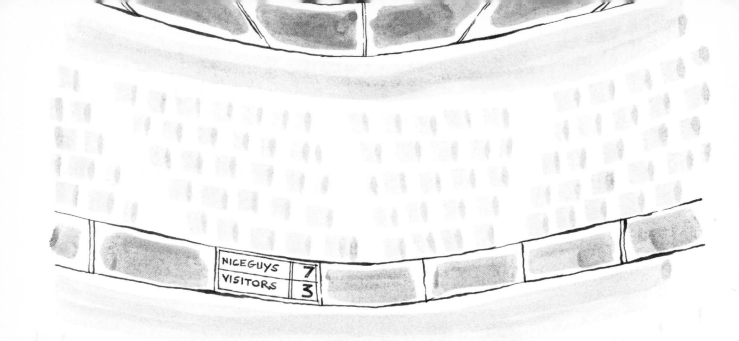

Besides hitting home runs and making great catches, Baseball Bob always took the time to sign autographs for all of his fans before and after each game.

One day, Little Billy's Dad had an idea.

"Billy, why don't you write a letter to Baseball Bob?"

11

"Great idea!" said Little Billy. "Then maybe he'll send me a picture." After Little Billy finished his homework and his chores, he took out his pencil, which was shaped like a baseball bat, and started to write.

Dear Baseball Bob,

You are my favorite baseb—all player. When I grow up, I hope to be as good as you. Could you please send me a picture of you so I can put it on my Wall of Favorite Pictures?

Thank you very much.

Your fan,

Little Billy

X X X

When he finished writing the letter, Little Billy walked to the post office with his Mom so he could send his letter to Baseball Bob.

Little Billy checked the mailbox every day to see if Baseball Bob's picture had arrived.

15

Two weeks went by without
mail from Baseball Bob.

One day, the doorbell rang. When Little Billy's Mom answered the door, she saw the mailman holding an envelope.

"I have a Special Delivery for Little Billy from the Niceguys!" the mailman said.

Little Billy's Mom took the envelope and thanked the mailman.

"Billy, there's something for you from the Niceguys!"
she called out.

Little Billy dashed over to his Mom. All he could think about was how his Wall of Favorite Pictures would look with the shiny new picture of his baseball hero right in the center.

When Little Billy opened the envelope, he found a letter from Baseball Bob, and even two tickets to a Niceguys game, but no picture! Little Billy was very happy about getting tickets, but he was also a little sad.

"Cheer up," said Billy's Dad. "At least we'll get to see Baseball Bob at the game."

When the day of the game arrived, Little Billy was very excited. He couldn't wait to see his baseball hero play. His Dad packed a camera and off to the stadium they went.

They arrived a little early, so Little Billy and his Dad decided to look for Baseball Bob to try and take his picture. Suddenly, they saw a big crowd around one of the players. It was Baseball Bob, signing autographs for all of the children. Sadly for Little Billy, the crowd was so big that he and his Dad could not get through to take Baseball Bob's picture.

The game was about to begin. Little Billy and his Dad found their seats. They cheered each time Baseball Bob got a hit, or made a catch, and cheered especially loudly when the Niceguys won the game!

It was time to go home. Little Billy's Dad could see the disappointment on his son's face.

"Don't worry Billy. Maybe next time we can get a picture of Baseball Bob."

Just as they were
about to leave, an
announcement came
over the loudspeaker.

"Attention please! Will
Little Billy and his Dad
please come to the
Niceguys dugout?"

Excitedly, Little Billy and his Dad raced to the Niceguys dugout, where a nice lady greeted them.

"Are you Little Billy and his Dad? Come with me, please. I have a surprise for you."

The nice lady led them into a room where there stood, none other than, Baseball Bob.

"Wow, you're Baseball Bob, my favorite baseball player!" said Little Billy. "Can my Dad please take a picture of you?"

"I've got a better idea," said Baseball Bob. "Why don't you stand next to me so your Dad can take a picture of the two of us together." Little Billy ran to Baseball Bob's side. They both said "cheese" as Little Billy's Dad snapped the picture.

After his Dad took the picture, Little Billy turned to Baseball Bob and asked, "How did you know we would be here today?"

"Your father called and told me about your letter and your Wall of Favorite Pictures. He also told me that the Niceguys sent you tickets to today's game."

"Thanks, Baseball Bob. You're my hero."

"You're welcome, Billy," said Baseball Bob. "But the real hero is your Dad. Without him, none of this would have happened!"

Little Billy and his Dad shook Baseball Bob's hand, said goodbye, and left the stadium to go home.

As they were driving home, Little Billy
turned to his father and said, "I love you,
Dad. Baseball Bob is a great baseball
player, but you are my real hero!"

"I love you too, Billy. Now let's go home and
hang that picture!"

ABOUT THE AUTHOR

Mitchell Axelrod was born in Queens, New York in 1962. A lifelong New York Mets fan, Mitchell overcame multiple physical disabilities in order to play, and excel at, the game of baseball. His first published book in 1999 was the critically acclaimed "Beatletoons – The Real Story Behind The Cartoon Beatles."

Mitchell was married in 2001 to Nancy. The happy couple were blessed with their first child, Spencer, in 2002. Mitchell hopes to share his love of "America's Pastime" with his son for many years to come.

ABOUT THE ILLUSTRATOR

Australian born U.S. citizen, **Ron Campbell** has spent 45 years in cartoon animation as a producer, director, animator, and storyboard artist. He produced and directed the animation for The Big Blue Marble, a children's TV show that won the prestigious George Foster Peabody Award in 1976, along with an Emmy for best children's show, and an Action for Children's Television award. He has been involved in the production of numerous television series, including Ed, Edd, and Eddy; The Rugrats; Rocket Power; The Smurfs; Captain Caveman; The Jetsons; The Flintstones; The Yellow Submarine; and, the show that brought him into contact with Mitch Axelrod, The Beatles Cartoon Series.

Ron lives in Carefree, Arizona, with his wife of 40 years, Engelina. They have two daughters and five grandchildren.